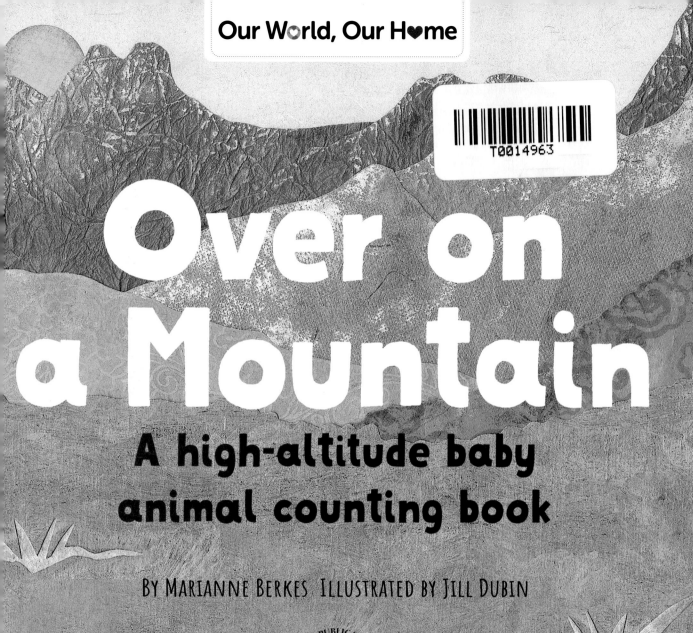

Over on a Mountain

A high-altitude baby animal counting book

By Marianne Berkes   Illustrated by Jill Dubin

DAWN PUBLICATIONS
CONNECTING CHILDREN AND NATURE

Over on a mountain,
grazing in the morning sun,
lived a woolly mother llama
and her little cria **one**.

"Roll," said the mother.
"I roll," said the **one**.
So they rolled in the dirt,
grazing in the morning sun.

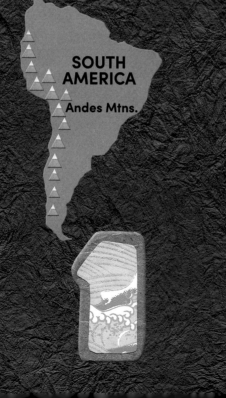

SOUTH
AMERICA

Andes Mtns.

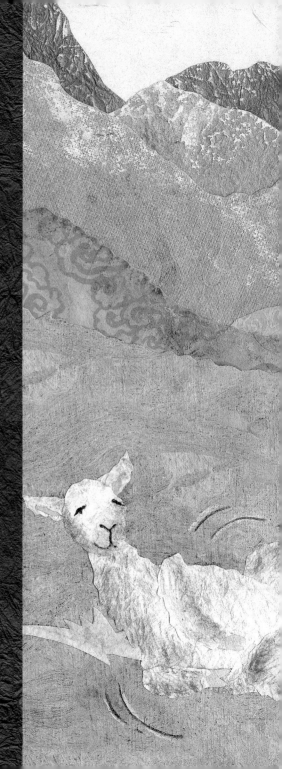

Over on a mountain,
where the bamboo grew,
lived a giant mother panda
and her little cubs **two**.

"Eat," said the mother.
"We eat," said the **two**.
So they ate, ate, and ate
where the bamboo grew.

ASIA

Min Mtns.

Over on a mountain,
near an evergreen tree,
lived a mother Alpine ibex
and her little kids **three**.

"Climb," said the mother.
"We climb," said the **three**.
So they climbed on a ledge
near an evergreen tree.

EUROPE

Alps

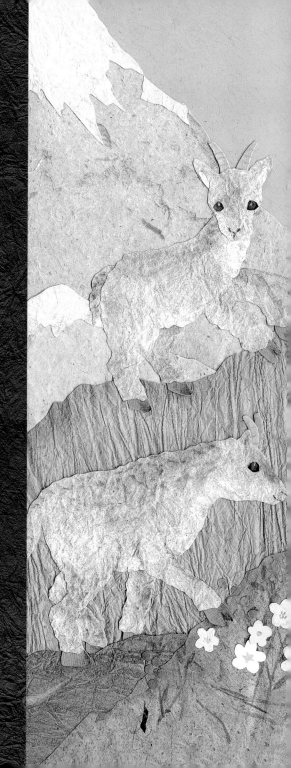

Over on a mountain,
where they often would snore,
lived a stocky mother wombat
and her little joeys **four**.

"Sleep," said the mother.
"We sleep," said the **four**.
So they slept in their burrow,
where they often would snore.

AUSTRALIA

Blue Mtns.

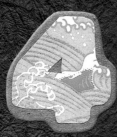

Over on a mountain,
where leaves and berries thrive,
lived a shy mother gorilla
and her little babies **five**.

"Forage," said the mother.
"We forage," said the **five**.
So they foraged in a forest
where leaves and berries thrive.

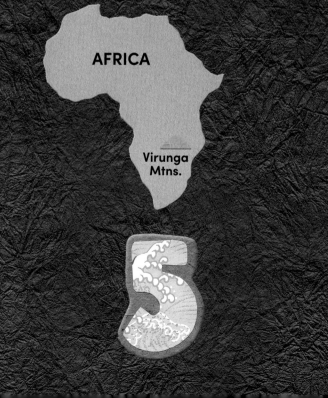

AFRICA

Virunga
Mtns.

Over on a mountain,
climbing over rocks and sticks,
lived a mother snow leopard
and her little cubs **six**.

"Leap," said the mother.
"We leap," said the **six**.
So they leaped way up high,
climbing over rocks and sticks.

ASIA

Himalayas

Over on a mountain,
gliding up toward the heavens,
lived a huge mother eagle
and her little eaglets **seven**.

"Soar," said the mother.
"We soar," said the **seven**.
So they soared with the wind,
gliding up toward the heavens.

Alaska Range

NORTH AMERICA

7

Over on a mountain,
where she knew how to wait,
lived a mother mountain lion
and her little cubs **eight**.

"Pounce," said the mother.
"We pounce," said the **eight**.
So they pounced on their prey,
where they knew how to wait.

NORTH AMERICA

Rocky Mtns.

8

Over on a mountain,
where the sun does shine,
lived a friendly mother yak
and her little calves **nine**.

"Huddle," said the mother.
"We huddle," said the **nine**.
So they huddled in the cold,
where the sun does shine.

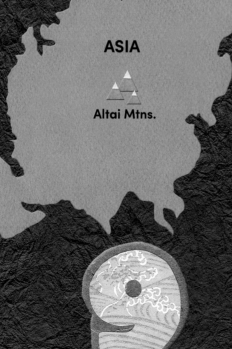

ASIA

Altai Mtns.

Over on a mountain,
with his mate, a female hen,
lived a father emperor penguin
and his little chicks **ten**.

"Waddle," said the father.
"We waddle," said the **ten**.
So they waddled on the ice
with their mom, a female hen.

ANTARCTICA

Trans-Antarctic Range

Over on a mountain,
living wild, living free,
as you look upon each page
count the babies that you see.

Some live on the mountains
that are in the USA.
Others live on continents
very far away.

Once you've named the continents,
then spy with your eyes
to find a hidden creature—
every page has a surprise!

Alaska
Range

NORTH
AMERICA

Rocky
Mtns.

ASIA

Altai Mtns.

Min Mtns.

Himalayan Mtns.

EUROPE

Alps

AFRICA

Virunga
Mtns.

SOUTH
AMERICA

Andes
Mtns.

AUSTRALIA
Blue
Mtns.

ANTARCTICA

Trans-Antarctic Range

Fact or Fiction?

In this variation of the song "Over in the Meadow," all the mountain animals actually behave as they have been portrayed. Snow leopards leap, bald eagles soar, and penguins waddle. That's a fact! But do they have the number of babies as in this rhyme? No! That is fiction. Emperor penguins only have one chick, not ten as in this story, and mountain gorillas usually have just one baby, not five. Do the babies live in the mountains shown in this book? Yes, they live where shown on the map, but sometimes live in other places too.

Baby animals are cared for in many different ways. Male snow leopards take no part in raising or protecting their cubs. But both mother and father eagle take care of their eaglets (usually one to three babies) until they are no longer helpless. And penguin males play a very unusual and important part in the birthing process. Nature has very different ways of ensuring the survival of different species.

Mountain Facts

Mountains can be found on all seven continents. They rise above the surrounding land, usually in the form of a peak. Mountain ranges are formed very slowly by movements of the Earth's crust. The height of a mountain is usually measured as the distance above sea level. The tallest mountain in the world above sea level is Mount Everest at 8,848 meters. Almost every country in the world uses the metric system, measuring in meters, not feet. In the United States, however, Mount Everest would be 29,029 feet above sea level. But if you were to measure from the base of a mountain (which may be on the floor of the ocean) to the top, the highest mountain would not be Mt. Everest—it's Mauna Kea in Hawaii, at 10,100 meters or 33,100 feet.

In general, the higher you go, the colder it is. To say this another way, temperature decreases as elevation increases—about 5.4 degrees colder for every 1000 feet gained in elevation. For example, if the temperature is 90 degrees Fahrenheit at the base of a mountain, it will be approximately 74 degrees Fahrenheit if you go 3000 feet up the mountain. So is every high mountain a very cold place? Well, not necessarily. Temperature also depends on where in the world the mountain is. A high mountain near the equator, where it is generally hot, will be a lot warmer than an equally high mountain in Antarctica or Alaska! All of this is very important because animals depend on plants for food, and few plants are hardy enough to grow at very high altitudes. Many animals will live high on mountains during the summer, but move downhill during the winter to find food.

The "Hidden" Animals

Chinchillas are rodents that are slightly larger than ground squirrels. They live together in colonies, making their dens in burrows and among rocks. Chinchillas have soft dense fur to protect them from the cold weather of the high Andes Mountains.

Golden eagles are raptors with beautiful gold feathers on the backs of their heads. They can be found in arid areas where there is little water, pursuing small mammals with their powerful beaks and talons, unlike bald eagles which are found near water and mainly hunt fish.

Marmots are large squirrels that live in burrows in mountainous areas such as the Alps. They are very social and use loud whistles to communicate with each other. They are herbivores that eat mainly grasses, lichens, and mosses.

Sugar gliders are small tree-dwelling marsupials with fox-like ears and big eyes. They have two thin flaps of skin that span from the fifth finger to the first toe on each side of their bodies, which allows them to glide through the air from tree to tree.

Grey-throated barbets are plump-looking solitary birds with large heads. They can be found in mountainous areas where they feed on fruit. They also eat a wide range of insects including ants and beetles.

Jumping spiders eat glacier fleas and springtails (insect-like creatures that are not true fleas but are among the most populous creatures on Earth!) which have, in turn, eaten tiny bits of vegetation and pollen blown up to the Himalayas from many miles away. They spend the night frozen, waiting for heat from the sun to revive them in the daytime when they jump and scavenge for food.

Moose are the largest members of the deer family. They are strong runners with hoofed feet and long legs. Only the males (bulls) have antlers which drop off each year and regrow the following year. The biggest moose antlers in North America come from Alaska and the Yukon Territory.

Bighorn sheep are hoofed mammals named for their large horns. They are closely related to goats and gather in large herds most of the year. Bighorn sheep live in mountain ranges from the Rocky Mountains in Colorado to southern Canada.

Mountain Apollo butterflies live on steep-sided slopes of high altitude mountains and tolerate a changing climate of dry summers and cold, snowy winters. This beautiful white butterfly is decorated with "eye" spots and shiny wings with transparent edges.

Arctic terns are the champion long-distance travelers of the animal world, traveling over 20,000 miles each year. When days grow shorter in the Arctic, they fly to Antarctica where summer is just starting so they can live in almost constant sunshine all through the year.

About the Animals

Llamas (also pronounced "yamas") are woolly mammals related to camels. Llamas are used as pack animals that have been helping people carry things across the Andes Mountains in South America for thousands of years. Llamas are alert and curious with keen senses of smell, hearing, and sight. They are herbivores—they eat mostly grasses and plant material. They like to roll in the dirt, taking dust baths that help maintain their fluffy wool coats. Baby llamas are called crias.

Pandas are giant bears that have lived for almost three million years in the bamboo forests of mountain ranges in central China, including the Min Mountains. Different from other bears, they have cat-like eyes and front paws with clawed fingers that grasp bamboo shoots and leaves, which they eat all day long. They use their powerful jaws and strong teeth to crush the tough bamboo into bits. Because bamboo is very low in nutrition, pandas need to consume about forty pounds of it every day. Young pandas are called cubs.

The Alpine ibex is a kind of wild goat that lives among the forests and high rocky areas of the European Alps. They climb steep slopes to feed on grass and flowers that grow in meadows or among the rocks. They also eat lichens and mosses that grow on stones. The rocky ledges protect them from predators. In the winter, when there is a lot of snow, they move to steep slopes where snow cannot pile up. Baby wild goats are called kids. Both male and females have horns.

Wombats live in underground burrows in the Blue Mountains of Australia. They have flat, wide paws with long, curved claws. As marsupials, their pouch is distinctive because it opens facing the mother's back legs. This prevents dirt from covering her baby while the mother is digging. The joey stays in the pouch until it can walk on its own. Wombats are nocturnal, meaning they come out at night to eat grasses, leaves, and roots. They spend the day in the sleeping chamber of their burrow, lying on their backs with their legs in the air, often snoring as they sleep.

Mountain gorillas are large, shy apes with thick fur that keeps them warm in the Virunga Mountains of Africa. They live in troops of six or seven females and young males, with only one adult male (a silverback) heading the group. They eat leaves, fruit, and occasionally termites and ants. They forage for food during the day and sleep at night in bowl-shaped "nests" made out of leaves. The mother shares a nest with her nursing baby and nurtures it for three or four years. Females have one baby at a time. Mountain gorillas are on the verge of extinction—only about six hundred of them remain.

Snow leopards are athletic wild cats that live in the very high, cold Himalayas, mostly in Tibet. Their ears are small, which helps them retain body heat. Their large paws act as snowshoes, and their long furry tails help them balance on rocky terrain. Snow leopards are carnivores that primarily hunt wild sheep and goats, but also ambush unsuspecting smaller animals. They can leap up to thirty feet—six times their body length—with their powerful hind legs. The mother usually gives birth to one to five cubs that are blind and helpless at birth and already have a thick coat of fur.

Bald eagles aren't really bald. They got that name because their white-feathered heads contrast with their brown bodies and wings. Female eagles are larger than males. Bald eagles are usually found near water abundant with fish, although they also capture other animals with their powerful talons. About half of the world's bald eagles live in Alaska, including the Alaska Range, but they can also be found throughout most of North America. Bald eagles soar using rising currents of warm air ("thermals") or up-drafts generated by terrain such as mountain slopes. Baby eagles are called eaglets.

Mountain lions are fierce, slender cats that hunt both day and night. Excellent jumpers and climbers, they often stalk their prey and ambush it by leaping from a tree. In the Rocky Mountains of North America, they kill larger animals by pouncing on their backs and breaking their necks. These fast, solitary carnivores can reach speeds of forty miles per hour as they chase prey such as deer. Female mountain lions have a special call to let males know they are ready to mate. After they do, the male goes his separate way and takes no part in raising the litter of one to three cubs that are born in a protected den.

Yaks are massive, shaggy-haired mammals who live high in the Altai Mountains of Central Asia, where there is a lot of sunshine. They are herbivores and graze on grasses and wildflowers. In winter, they use their dense horns to break through snow to eat the plants beneath. The high elevation makes their habitat very cold and windy, but the wild yaks' dense fur keeps in body heat so they can live in temperatures of negative 40 degrees Fahrenheit. They gather in large herds and huddle together to protect themselves from the cold and from predators, with their young calves in the center. Yaks are related to cattle and were domesticated hundreds of years ago to help humans pull heavy loads through mountain passes.

Emperor penguins are birds that cannot fly. They are great swimmers, however, and spend most of their lives at sea. Many live on Antarctic pack ice in colonies at the base of the Transantarctic Mountains that stretch across the continent. During the coldest time of the year, the female penguin lays a single egg and the male incubates it for about seventy days, balancing it on his feet under a warm flap of skin called a "brood pouch." Meanwhile, the female finds krill, squid, and fish in the ocean for her family, and eventually waddles her way back on the ice to feed her chick. Penguins waddle because their feet are set so far back on their bodies.

Tips from the Author

ACTIVITIES

Sing and Act: While you sing, act out what each animal does: roll, climb, soar, waddle, and so on. Kids can also make masks of the animals and wear them as they enjoy the story.

Fun with Words: Introduce vocabulary words in the story that younger children might not be familiar with, e.g. cria, ibex, forage, prey, huddle, continent, equator, bamboo, and ask kids to find the words in the story.

Where Do They Live? Using animal printouts (See EnchantedLearning.com), color and cut out each animal that is in the story. Draw or download a map of all the continents. Children can place their animal on the correct continent.

Who Am I? Write two sentences describing an animal in this book without identifying the animal. Have kids guess the animal. E.g., "I am different from other bears. I eat bamboo all day long."

CONSTRUCT AN ATTRIBUTE CHART

On the top horizontal sections of a grid, enter category headings: Continent, Animal Name, and Baby Name for students to fill in after reading the story. Younger children can use a three-column chart, while older students can add other columns such as action (what they are doing in the story) what they eat (are they omnivores, carnivores or herbivores?) and are they nocturnal or diurnal?

RESEARCH THE MOUNTAINS

Which mountain is the highest? Where is it located? What are some other mountains on that continent that are among the highest mountains in the world? How high is the highest mountain on each continent? You can draw a grid for this also, labeling the headings: Continent, Name of Mountain, and Height. Older students may want to use two columns for the height (feet and meters).

GOIN' TO THE ZOO. HOW ABOUT YOU?

Spend a day with family and friends observing zoo animals. Make a list of the animals in this book and see how many you can find at your zoo. What a great way to teach kids about respect for living creatures. Each time you go, you will share unique experiences that can last a lifetime.

COMPARE AND CONTRAST

In a Venn diagram, compare the hidden animal to the main animal on each page. How are they the same and how are they different? Describe their body parts, how they move, what they eat, sounds they make, and so on.

Tips from the Artist

In their natural habitat, animals use camouflage to blend into their environment. This is usually to protect themselves and their young from predators. Within each illustration, there is a hidden animal for you to find. Some are easy to spot and some take a little more searching. As the illustrator, it's always a challenge for me to come up with ways to hide these creatures.

Just as color and texture help animals blend into their surrounding areas, I use the same idea in my illustrations. Each illustration is a collage using cut paper with pastel and colored pencil for details. I have a lot of wonderful papers with a wide range of colors and patterns and textures. I chose each paper carefully, thinking about how it will look when all of the pieces are put together. When I'm planning the illustration, I keep the hidden element in mind. I try different papers to see what will help it blend into the background.

One morning when I went out to water my clematis plant, I noticed a newt perched on the edge of the planter. I took a picture of it before it scurried away. I used that photo to show how changing the background of a picture either makes the newt easy to see or much more difficult to spot.

The first photo on the left is exactly as I took it. In the second photo, I isolated the newt so I could try different backgrounds. As you can see, some of the backgrounds make the newt stand out and some make it very hard to find.

There are lots of hidden creatures in our environment—a green grasshopper on a blade of grass, a brown sparrow on a branch, or a gray bunny among the underbrush. You may be able to see some hidden animals in your neighborhood if you keep still and look all around you.

Over on a Mountain

Sung to the tune
"Over in the Meadow"

Traditional tune
Words by Marianne Berkes

2. Over on a mountain, where the bamboo grew,
   lived a giant mother panda and her little cubs two.
   "Eat," said the mother. "We eat," said the two.
   So they ate, ate, and ate where the bamboo grew.

3. Over on a mountain, near an evergreen tree,
   lived a mother Alpine ibex and her little kids three.
   "Climb," said the mother. "We climb," said the three.
   So they climbed on a ledge near an evergreen tree.

4. Over on a mountain, where they often would snore,
   lived a stocky mother wombat and her little joeys four.
   "Sleep," said the mother. "We sleep," said the four.
   So they slept in their burrow, where they often would snore.

5. Over on a mountain, where leaves and berries thrive,
   lived a shy mother gorilla and her little babies five.
   "Forage," said the mother. "We forage," said the five.
   So they foraged in a forest where leaves and berries thrive.

6. Over on a mountain, climbing over rocks and sticks,
   lived a mother snow leopard and her little cubs six.
   "Leap," said the mother. "We leap," said the six.
   So they leaped way up high, climbing over rocks and sticks.

7. Over on a mountain, gliding up toward the heavens,
   lived a huge mother eagle and her little eaglets seven.
   "Soar," said the mother. "We soar," said the seven.
   So they soared with the wind, gliding up toward
   the heavens.

8. Over on a mountain, where she knew how to wait,
   lived a mother mountain lion and her little cubs eight.
   "Pounce," said the mother. "We pounce," said the eight.
   So they pounced on their prey, where they knew how
   to wait.

9. Over on a mountain, where the sun does shine,
   lived a friendly mother yak and her little calves nine.
   "Huddle," said the mother. "We huddle," said the nine.
   So they huddled in the cold, where the sun does shine.

10. Over on a mountain, with his mate, a female hen,
    lived a father emperor penguin and his little chicks ten.
    "Waddle," said the father. "We waddle," said the ten.
    So they waddled on the ice with their mom, a female hen.

Marianne Berkes has spent much of her life as an early childhood educator, children's theater director, and children's librarian. She is the award-winning author of over twenty-three interactive picture books that make learning fun. Her books, inspired by her love of nature, open kids' eyes to the magic found in our natural world. Marianne hopes young children will want to read each book again and again, each time learning something new and exciting. Her website is MarianneBerkes.com.

Jill Dubin's whimsical art has appeared in over thirty children's books. Her cut-paper illustrations reflect her interest in combining color, pattern, and texture. She grew up in Yonkers, New York, and graduated from Pratt Institute. She lives with her family in Cape Cod, including two dogs that do very little but with great enthusiasm. Visit her at JillDubin.com.

For the Coblentz boys. May you always have a sense of wonder!
—MB

In loving memory of my father, who climbed the heights and sailed the seas.
—JD

Published by Dawn Publications, an imprint of Sourcebooks eXplore
P.O. Box 4410, Naperville, Illinois 60567–4410
(630) 961-3900
sourcebookskids.com

Originally published in 2015 in the United States by Dawn Publications.

Library of Congress Cataloging-in-Publication Data is on file with the publisher.

Source of Production: Wing King Tong Paper Products Co. Ltd., Shenzhen, Guangdong Province, China
Date of Production: July 2021
Run Number: 5020848

Printed and bound in China.
WKT 10 9 8 7 6 5 4 3 2 1

ALSO BY MARIANNE BERKES AND DAWN PUBLICATIONS

Baby on Board: How Animal Parents Carry their Young — These are some of the clever ways animals carry their babies!

Over in the Ocean — With unique and outstanding style, this book portrays a vivid community of marine creatures.

Over in the Jungle — As with *Ocean*, this book captures a rain forest teeming with remarkable animals.

Over in the Arctic — Another charming counting rhyme introduces creatures of the tundra.

Over in the Forest — Follow the tracks of forest animals, but watch out for the skunk!

Over in Australia — Australian animals are often unique, many with pouches for the babies. Such fun!

Over in a River — Beavers, manatees, and so many more animals help teach the geography and habitats of ten great North American rivers.

Over in the Grasslands — Come along on a safari! Lions, rhinos, and hippos introduce the African Savanna.

Over on the Farm — Welcome to the farm, where pigs roll, goats nibble, horses gallop, hens peck, and turkeys strut! Count, clap, and sing along.

Over on a Desert — Camels, tortoises, roadrunners, and jerboas help teach the habitat of the desert.

Going Around the Sun: Some Planetary Fun — Earth is part of a fascinating "family" of planets.

Going Home: The Mystery of Animal Migration — A book that is an introduction to animals that migrate.

Seashells by the Seashore — Kids discover, identify, and count twelve beautiful shells to give Grandma for her birthday.

The Swamp Where Gator Hides — Still as a log, only his watchful eyes can be seen.

What's in the Garden? — Good food doesn't begin on a store shelf in a box. It comes from a garden bursting with life!

OTHER NATURE BOOKS FROM DAWN PUBLICATIONS

Tall Tall Tree — Take a peek at some of the animals that make their home in a tall, tall tree—a magnificent coast redwood. Rhyming verses and a one-to-ten counting scheme made this a real page-turner.

Daytime Nighttime, All Through the Year — Delightful rhymes depict two animals for each month, one active during the day and one busy at night. See all the action!

Octopus Escapes Again! — Swim along with Octopus as she searches for food. Will she eat or be eaten? She outwits dangerous enemies by using a dazzling display of defenses.

Paddle, Perch, Climb: Bird Feet Are Neat — Become a bird detective as you meet the feet that help birds eat—so many different shapes, sizes, and ways to use them. It's time for lunch!

Dandelion Seed's Big Dream — A charming tale that follows a seed as it floats from the countryside to the city and encounters all sorts of obstacles and opportunities.

A Moon of My Own — An adventurous young girl journeys around the world accompanied by her faithful companion, the Moon. Wonder and beauty await you.